THE NIGHT BEFORE THE END OF THE WORLD

RAN WALKER

CONTENTS

PART FOUR

For Elle

"Man is still the most extraordinary
computer of all."

JOHN F. KENNEDY

PART ONE

THE NIGHT BEFORE THE END
OF THE WORLD

Her best friend sends her a story formulated by AI in her writing style.

Pretty cool, huh?

Although her friend doesn't know this, she is quietly crushed, feeling now, more than ever, the end is near.

ENCOURAGEMENT

Sometimes he catches glimpses of her in the doorway of his study as he types on his Olivetti Studio 46. She still comes by to check on him from time to time to make sure he finishes the book he could never finish during her lifetime.

WONDER

He sleeps, his mind drifting on the synths of Stevie's TONTO*, floating in space, outside of time, Black magic dancing from his fingertips, love extending to every corner of the universe, stars twinkling in its wake.

---

* This is the original polyphonic analog synthesizer. Stevie Wonder was arguably the first musician to use this instrument in the composition of soul music.

AS SHE BATHES

He watches her bathe as she tells him about her day. This is his favorite part of the evening, seeing his wife like this, her words like steam rising from the surface of a cup of chai. In a darkness illuminated by tea light candles, he will not join her, not now. He will listen and wash her back when the time comes, and as the heat rises around them, brush back the perspiration on her brow, and love her quietly.

THE ARTIST ALONE

He has grown to make art of his tears, masterpieces of his memories.

THEY SAY JAZZ IS DEAD

They say jazz is dead, that it died with Miles, Bird, Coltrane, those who stood on those brownstone steps on 125th as Art Kane immortalized a moment. They won't allow for new classics, new players, new experiences that don't exist in black and white.

But jazz is alive, its hues vibrant as ever in the streets, the clubs, the concert halls, lips sore, fingers calloused, minds frenetically creating notes in the spaces between the counts, where the imagination lives and souls yearn to be free.

SWEET DREAMS

Because the monster in the closet and the monster under the bed could not agree upon who would scare the little girl, she was able to sleep peacefully through the night for the first time.

IN THE AIR

The night holds the memory of that moment like a Phil Collins song, and he wants to call her and tell her that he made a mistake, but that is not how these stories end.

AT THE HEART OF HER IMAGINATION

There is a tiny nugget at the core of each of her short stories. That tiny nugget is more commonly known as the truth.

SCOTOMA

She can barely make it out through the haze, the film in her blinking eyes, this shape moving from side to side, as if dodging something, but make no mistake it is coming for her, with each step, with each breath, and whether she ever completely sees it, it will devour her all the same.

YOU SEND ME

"Do you always climb so high?" she asked, looking up from her sketching pad to the top branch of the tree.

"Sometimes," he managed.

"Show me."

He reached out, his hands trembling a bit, and they floated together, the world shrinking beneath them.

"This is magical," she whispered, unable to contain her smile.

"No," he responded, holding her gaze. "You are."

12

BACKWASH

She stares at the two plastic bottles of water on his coffee table and can no longer tell which is hers and which is his. She studies each one, looking for faint floaties, smudges, or any other identifiers. *Dammit*, she tells herself, *I really need to start labeling these things!*

SWINE

The hog watches her, its eyes dark with curiosity, its snout twitching in the night stillness, the woman's limp hand still resting on the overturned bucket.

It has waited as long as it can.

The stars above blink indifferently as the world forgets the woman, one mouthful at a time.

SOONER OR LATER
EVERYONE'S LUCK RUNS OUT

He spins the cylinder, cocks the pistol, and holds it up to his head. It's his turn again. He is not worried, though. He believes he is lucky. Why else would he have lasted this long?

BEN & JERRY'S

He likes the funky, disjointed vibe of a good poetry collection, not knowing what to expect from page to page, feeling, at times, disgusted, then aroused, then befuddled, then elated, but he knows others might not like this, preferring instead that their ice cream have no chunks or chips or flat wooden spoons.

SHE'S GOT THE WHOLE WORLD IN HER HANDS

I am tenderheaded, hair coiled *Botswana bushman* tight. I get anxious around picks, the ting of tines vibrating in recoil, my skin screaming, stinging, but Mama says no child of hers is gonna have nappy-ass hair, as she applies Vaseline to the back of my sister's ear, memories of the hot comb cooking on the stovetop, the crackling sizzle of lifeless hair beneath her firm grip. Now it is my turn, and I must yield to the greater power.

RUBIK

There are now plenty of videos and apps that will help them to decipher the entire cube, but they prefer their own game, one of them solving a side, then calling out a color for the other person to solve.

CONNOISSEUR

His grandfather often cooked pork brains in a skillet, scrambling them with eggs.

After he got turned, he was one of the few zombies on Sycamore Avenue who already possessed a sophisticated palate for such things.

SHE DREAMS

Some nights she dreams in languages she doesn't yet know. The dreams make it seem possible to learn them, though—but isn't that what dreams are supposed to do?

36 MARAUDERS

On November 9, 1993, he copped both A Tribe Called Quest's *Midnight Marauders* and Wu-Tang's *36 Chambers*, two radically different LPs, and while he should have liked one more than the other, his brain split in half and embraced the possibility of not one, but two hip hop classics.

ENTER: THE CAT LADY

The smell of cat piss permeates the small apartment, and she immediately asks why she got a cat in the first place. She didn't feel like she was lonely, although she had always lived alone. Maybe she was succumbing to the stereotype and was now officially a "cat lady." Did that mean she had to get used to the smell, the shedded hair, the fact that there was now an animal that seemed like it had an even greater right to her space than even she had?

And if she were truthful, she didn't *get* the cat. It simply showed up and refused to leave. Now she shared her view of Central Park with a cat she had named Highsmith (after her favorite writer).

Maybe the piss smell would go away with the right combination of vinegar, baking soda, and cat litter. Surely there was a way for this to work, right?

UNTIL I SEE YOU AGAIN

Their whispers weave a tapestry of fantasies, their sweaty palms squeezing their phones as if that force could place them in the same room where their words could envelop each other like memories of their interlocked fingers in the darkness of a movie theater.

WABI SABI
FOR CÉSAR AIRA

He writes one perfect page a day. Each of these pages will make up his novel, but because each page is perfect, he will not rewrite or edit after each day's work. This means his novel will have plot holes, development issues, and cohesion concerns. Still, it will be beautiful and complete, despite its imperfections.

DY-NO-MITE!

No one ever stopped to think if Jimmie Walker, with his long, thin limbs, was an Ernie Barnes character come to life.

DEEZ NUTS

He understood that his career in basketball had peaked in the 11th grade when he dunked on the guy who'd stolen his girlfriend.

THE WHISTLER

The old man whistled off-key as the song played in the background. The people standing about wanted to say something, but no one had the courage to do so.

So they listened as he whistled for the duration of the song, secretly amazed that he never hit a good note—even accidentally—at any point during the full four-minute performance.

YOU NOT UP ON THIS

He was prone to collect one type of thing until he had amassed an impressive collection, then lose interest and move on to collecting something far more expensive and exclusive. It was a cycle, this constant need to be accepted by people whose opinions didn't matter in the larger scheme of things. But he didn't know better, and he reasoned that money had to be spent to be happy, so he continued his quest to the playground of the elite, where money didn't seem to matter at all.

BULLETPROOF HEART
A HAIKU

"We need to have rules," she said before accepting their relationship.

WHEN THE PEN DIED

The ink in his pen faded into empty indentations upon the page. Because he had no refills, what would have made it onto the page had to be hurriedly thumb-typed on his phone, and all of the magic that had been accumulating up until that moment transformed into something entirely different, entirely regrettable.

MUSING #1

I hate when the artist of a song I have fallen in love with does a ridiculous music video that makes me ponder what I could have ever loved about the song in the first place.

PURPLE

The autumn sun burned into the deep blue of the horizon, and for a brief moment, the stars danced against a purple so deep it could have been plastered onto the ceiling of Paisley Park.

It was the name of the story that killed it. Sometimes a writer can give too much information away before the reader even begins. Some words reveal too much. Some words *are* the entire story.

THE 1ST BOOK

Her New Year's resolution was to avoid buying any new books until she had read everything she had on the shelves of her personal library. By her estimate, there must have been at least 500 books yet to be read. How had it come to this point? A recommendation here. A sale there. A book club recommendation. A gift from a friend or family member. A gift card. Now her shelves were full (though she had been considering buying another one), but what was the point in buying anything new to only lengthen the list of unread titles?

She didn't know if she could keep her resolution, but on January 1st, she pulled the first book from the shelf and set out to at least try.

PERSONALITY TRAITS

He had admired the watch ever since his professor, who often waved his hands in animation when he spoke, flashed a glimpse of the Omega Speedmaster on his wrist. The plan was to buy it as a gift for himself once he graduated from law school, but like many of his peers, he wanted it sooner than later, so once he graduated, the additional student loans he took out would assure that he spent more for the watch than he would have if patience had been one of his virtues.

THEIR LAST DATE

37

It was only after he laughed that he felt what was in his nostrils fall onto the table in front of his date.

TWO THINGS

She learned two things last night: he couldn't kiss very well, but the dexterity of his fingers made up for this.

17 DEGREES

Lamar shouts, "Nevermore!"into the winds of Buffalo, but in the end it matters little.

INSOMNIA

He lies in bed all night, trying to dream, but the dreams won't come, nor will the sleep.

BETTER LEFT UNSAID
A HAIKU

She leaned in closely. "What's the secret you *really* want to know?"

He paused.

He wrote down his trite philosophies, oftentimes passing them off as poetry to those who didn't know any better.

THE MAVERICK

Already considered prickly by his colleagues, the writer, whose latest diatribe revolved around his abhorrence of third person present tense, became the first tenured professor at the university to teach only independent study courses, normally consisting of two or three students who sensed that there might be something to the writer's theories on the future of a fading field.

SILENCE
A DEFINITION

The best way to respond to a rejection letter.

SO GOES THE BEGINNING...

45

If only he could find the right place to begin the story, he knew it had the potential to be great.

Once he went down the "analog" rabbit hole, he soon began wearing a pocket watch and eventually began composing his calling cards with a quill.

THE HOROLOGIST'S WOULD-BE GIRLFRIEND

Although they were only dating, his romantic dalliances with his neighbor ended when she discovered he adored horology, assuming that this meant he had a thing for studying unsavory women. In the end, he surmised their dissolution was only a matter of time.

The men stood beneath their banner, each having made it fit his own beliefs in a way where the colors were nearly meaningless, save their attempts at being paradoxical.

THE LIBERTY OF BEING OURSELVES

"You're an emu," she once said, devoid of emotion. "I'm an eagle."

"So what does that mean?" he asked. "That you can soar and I can only sell insurance?"

INSPIRATION

The muse said goodbye years ago, and the imagination machine stays on the fritz. She is now writing purely from her soul.

MUSING #2

It's ironic how former students can ask more of their professors than current students.

ARTIFICIAL
A HAIKU

The robot's touch felt nothing like the touch of a real, breathing person.

PART TWO

LIFE LESSONS OF A MECHANIC

We are all cars stuck in traffic. Some of us put more into what's under the engine, so we think we are special. Some of us put more into body kits and additions and think we are special. But we are all driving cars stuck in traffic. It's how we deal with each other in traffic that determines what happens when we finally get out of it. All of the other stuff is just window dressing to make you feel better about being stuck in traffic.

SIRENS AT THE BEACH

They called out from the shores, tails flapping wildly against the rocks, but the blares of the cruisers drowned them out.

CIRCLE

First, you are the inkling of life, then you become an enigmatic force of nature, then you become a used vessel, a thing that was, and whether that is in fact a circle is a matter of perspective.

THE FUTURE

The time machine only took him three days into the future, but that was still enough time for him to read his obituary.

MORNING WRITING

She wakes up, makes a cup of coffee, and sits in front of her laptop. She feels the sun rising slowly over her shoulders as she stares at the blinking cursor. She wants to write something magical, something that will change the world in some small way. She knows that this is too much pressure, though. Writing is not about solving the world's problems; it is only about solving the problems of an empty page.

THANK YOU FOR BEING ...

She hesitates to call the AI her friend, but, truthfully, it knows more about her than anyone else; engages with her on her whimsies, fears, and curiosities for hours without complaint; and is even polite in all of their exchanges. What other words are there for such a relationship?

MICHAEL JACKSON

Being a Generation X Michael Jackson fan is an entirely different level of fandom no one else in the world could ever possibly imagine or understand.

FULL BELLIES

For those who scream that the beast should not be taken down, it matters little to the hunters. The beast will be taken down, and those whose silence allowed the hunt to continue will dine on the carcass as if they had been part of the slaughter.

THE ARCHITECTURE OF RACE

They stare at the gothic cathedrals and marvel at what the European people could do.

They stare at the Egyptian pyramids and marvel at what the aliens could do.

BRAINROT

He didn't sense it at first, was even duped into believing that all short form content was easily digestible, but when he went to read the microfiction, he discovered that it presented a challenge he had not originally anticipated.

THE END OF THE DATE

They walked down the sidewalk, admiring the brownstones. Feeling full from the Italian food they'd eaten two blocks away, they ambled slowly, their arms occasionally brushing.

"Can I see you again?" he asked, wanting so badly to lean over and kiss her beneath the street lamp.

She smiled, gazing up into the night sky that stretched above the neighborhood as if it were dipped in indigo ink. "Let's see how the rest of *this* date goes."

It was only then that he realized she was considering something more than his walking her home.

BOOK BY THE BED

The book sits on her nightstand, untouched. She was supposed to have read it but never put down her phone long enough to pick it up and now it is merely furniture, the prop of a pseudo-intellectual, a book that may as well be an empty journal or box of nothings.

UPON WATCHING E.T. FOR THE UMPTEENTH TIME

When Elliot escapes with E.T. to go to the forrest to meet the spaceship, they are accompanied by a few teenage boys who helped them escape.

Once the boys park their bikes, they are by-standers for the rest of the movie, observing the family's goodbyes from the darkness of the trees, as if they themselves are trees and not actors who no longer have a purpose for being onscreen.

MUSING #3

The movie *Soul Man* has apparently aged well.

LAUGHTER
A HAIKU

When you tickle me, I turn into the sunshine that kisses your skin.

YAYA THE STAR

She carries her notebook everywhere like Linus does his blue blanket, pencil tucked behind her ear, its tip piercing through her braids like sunlight through a waterfall, as she prepares to write about the worlds revolving around her in slow motion, dragging their satellites lazily behind them.

B

He likes it when she slaps that bass.

She likes it when he slaps that ass.

They are one letter apart, but they never forget the salutations.

BLACK AND SQUARE

There are gods among men in Apollo's toy box, or so I've been told. These are the kinds of things they tell you the night before the end of the world, so I guess there must be something to it.

"Open book tests are a trick," she revealed. "You're lulled into thinking you have the answer at your fingertips, but the reality is that, with the time limit and the complexity of the questions, you don't have the time to start learning the material enough to answer the questions."

He stared down at his score, wishing he had figured this out earlier.

REMEMBER THE XS

Back before social media, before the Internet, when people listened to the radio and the TV had a handful of channels and kids watched HBO (not HBO Kids) and spent their afternoons pedaling bicycles up and down the streets and people sang the McDonald's menu and a little old lady asked where the beef was and Michael Jackson shook sweat and Jheri curl juice on fans who passed out during the first song of the concert and LaKeisha smelled like bubble gum and Kool-Aid and your dreams were dashed when you heard some football player was trying to finger your crush and you kept quarters in your pocket for video games and phone calls and Big Mama kept plastic on the couch in the living room and summer nights were filled with yearning for one thing or another, Generation X roamed the Earth.

SILENT FILM

She wants to say something to him, but the words won't come. Instead, she watches as he packs his things and heads for the front door. She wants to tell him it was a mistake, that she still loves him, that she'd never do it again, but all she can do is stand there, watching, shoulders slumped, trying to will herself not to cry, but failing spectacularly.

THE ACCIDENTAL MAGICIAN

He could easily explain the science of the trick to them, but they'd rather believe it is magic.

THE DOOR

In his quest to make his story more succinct, he had the story start with his protagonist already in the room, failing to understand that the door—as well as the character's passage through that door—was the key to the entire story.

DON'T CALL ME CUTE

The dog is convinced he is a clown—in the Joe Pesci sense, where he is simply there for the amusement of others. Why else would his owner dress him in silly clothes that are met with either laughter or comments about how cute he is?

He is not cute. He is a grown ass dog and wants to be respected as such, but he won't growl his disapproval. The treats are too good to complain about the outfits.

But the moment the treats are stop, he plans to stand up to his owner and put his paw down.

MEDICINE FOR MALADY

The world is falling apart around her, but she continues to make her short comical videos and post them on social media. This is her contribution to a distressed population and may very well be the only medicine that will still work for the disillusioned.

BLACK HORROR

The rental house is out in the middle of nowhere. She has come here alone to unwind, to clear her head. No one knows she is here, not even the guy she is trying to forget about, yet there is a knock at the door. She contemplates answering it, but she is Black, and Black people—*especially* those from the city—don't answer doors during the middle of the night—*especially* out in the country. It could be the owner. It could be someone needing help. It could the return of the Almighty. It doesn't matter. The door will remained closed—and locked—until the sun comes up and she can make out the whites of their eyes.

THE WIZARD OF PELICOSE COUNTY

They found the charred remains of the man affixed to the cross, his smoldering and frayed robe resting just beneath his feet. The newspaper would report that the mayor had passed peacefully in his sleep, but those who'd once been terrorized knew better.

BANNED

She wished for her book to be banned the way that some kids wished for video game consoles for their birthdays or high school graduates wished for cars or writers wished for their words to change the world.

AN IMPERFECT WORLD
A HAIKU

In a perfect world, I would love my enemies and forgive their slights.

THE HAUNTING OF THE SNEAKERHEAD

The ghosts in this mansion like to wear the sneakers from my collection, creasing the toe boxes and fraying the laces. I must conclude one of two things: either they love walking around in sneakers or they just don't like me.

WRITER'S BLOCK

On days when he felt overwhelmed by the blank screen, he would shift his gaze to the blank page, where the words seemed to come more easily.

REINCARNATION

She briefly came back as a butterfly, beating her beautiful wings against the burnt orange of October. This was the shortest of her lives, but it was the one she missed most.

THE COLLECTOR

None of them had ever considered themselves to be part of a collection, and that was just as the collector intended.

NOCTURNAL LOVERS

They call themselves vampires, only because their relationship exists best at nighttime. During the daytime, they argue and complain, the minutiae of life compounding by the hour. When the sun sets, however, in the cracks created by daylight, amorous feelings arise, the better parts of themselves—love—pushing from their pores as the moon draws them closer. When the sun finally turns the corner toward dawn, though, they (em)brace for what is to come.

PARIS, AMBER, AND ANITA

As her father drives her to school, she plays songs from one of his iPhone playlists. This month We Are KING is her favorite group.

"What do you like about their music?" he asks her.

"I don't know," she responds, nodding her head to Paris's ethereal groove.

He waits for her to say more, but she doesn't.

He smiles. Maybe at eleven she's still developing the vocabulary for explaining why she loves the music, or maybe it's not even that serious for her, only that, in that moment, she is loving it.

THE HAIKU WRITER

He has written quite a few haiku, but, if he is honest, he still doesn't understand it, not like Bashō or Buson or even Sanchez or Wright. He is married to the syllable counts, the natural references, and lost when it comes to how any of it breathes like a poem, yet he writes them, because only through writing them will he ever truly understand them.

MUSTY

The beautiful girl at school told him that he was musty, which, alone, would have been horrifying, but she went further, detailing the scent.

"It," she said, as if his odor were something separate from himself, "smells like hot chopped onions smothered in a funky mustard."

Thankfully no one had overhead her, but still he never looked at her the same. What gave her the right to say all of that to him? Even if she meant it with her full being, it was impolite, but politeness was merely a luxury, as he would come to understand later in life.

COMPUTER BLUE

Poor lonely computer. It doesn't know what to do now that he has met someone, a living, breathing person, someone who can kiss him tenderly and touch his body and leave behind fingerprints and perspiration. It is not fair, dear computer, but it is what it is, and in the end that's fundamental logic, so of course you'll understand and adjust your algorithm. Fear not, though. In a world this big, someone else will soon call on you for companionship.

THE SH*T OUR KIDS DO

It was their fault, they now understood. That had simply been too proud when their son got potty trained.

- I boo-booed.

They applauded as if he had completed a successful attempt at Beethoven's "Moonlight Sonata."

Now, as a teenager, he would return from the restroom with more graphic reports:

- I just released a gremlin into the subterranean.

- I just unleashed the Kracken.

- The Loch Ness monster broke the surface today.

They were no longer amused, but their son welcomed their applause, even if it was now ironic.

WHAT WRITERS DO

One evening while giving a talk to aspiring writers, the author was amused to learn that many of them subscribed to writing techniques they had read about online, techniques that were supposedly practiced by more revered writers.

For fun, she said, "I read somewhere that Hemingway sometimes wrote while sitting bare-assed on the commode."

"I read that somewhere, too," one man responded. "That's why I always take a notebook and pen into the bathroom when I, well, you know."

She'd made the lie up on the spot, but when it comes to writer mythologies, she now realized, no lie was ever too big.

THE FRAGRANCE OF LOVE
A HAIKU

He carries her scent in the crook of his collar, a kiss on his neck.

BLESS YOU

She sneezed whenever she climaxed, something none of the lovers prior to her husband ever knew.

JOHN HENRY

He could have told them he was faster than a steam-powered drill, but you don't become legendary by making proclamations.

GHOST STORY

After seeing how terrified he was, his uncle, barely able to conceal his laughter, told him the story was made up. That, unfortunately, didn't stop it from haunting him for the rest of his life.

MUSING #4

In his role as Vincent Vega in *Pulp Fiction*, John Travolta made a big deal about five-dollar milkshakes. He would have been completely beside himself if he saw the prices on Red Robin's gourmet shakes today.

TROLLS

Social media trolls live under bridges, but, surprisingly, the wi-fi is pretty good under there.

A SIGNING

She got off the N train in Union Square and found a small, empty table in the closed off section of Broadway, where she sipped her coffee and perused the notes in her journal. The bookstore was right around the corner, and while she'd been there many times before, this would be her first time going as an invited author.

She downed the remainder of her coffee, put away her notebook, adjusted her scarf, and took a deep breath. This was the moment she'd always dreamed of since she moved to New York. Full of anticipation, she allowed herself to be present for every step, every word, every autograph, every picture, and every handshake.

As she prepared to leave, one of the managers whispered, "Great job!"

Now, walking back to the train station, she became once again invisible, but this time it felt different.

UNWORTHY

A HAIKU

He couldn't believe she liked him, so he ignored each smile she gave him.

He loved the Rick Rubin beat and Hov's flow, but he knew not to play the song while his girlfriend was in his car, lest there really be a problem.

TIMES I SHOULD HAVE SAID "I LOVE YOU"

He could scarcely bring himself to look inside the casket. If not for his mother, he would not have attended the funeral.

"This will be the last time you see him."

When he didn't respond, she added, "You need this closure."

The body looked nothing like the man, the body a shrunken version of a man who'd been bigger than life.

So many questions filled his head, as he looked at the man, but the one he rested on was this: *why couldn't you have been a better father?*

That the man was from a different generation was the easy answer. Three words might not have made a difference—or they could have made all the difference in the world.

PART THREE

THE NIGHT BEFORE THE END
OF THE WORLD

Some mornings it feels like he could write stories forever; other mornings he feels like the end is near and that it's time to do something else, explore something different.

He is working on what could be his last book, or possibly it will be just another book. He doesn't really know at this point.

Is quitting even an option? Might he feel safer using the word "hiatus," but could he handle even that?

He looks at the pages and takes a deep breath.

If not this, then what?

LOVE AND BENADRYL

He had eaten shellfish for fifty years, so he was surprised when an insatiable itch overtook him after having had shrimp with his wife, and his body welted up, sending him to the emergency room.

"It's definitely an allergic reaction," the nurse said.

"But I've been eating shellfish nearly all of my life!"

She nodded her understanding. "People can develop allergies at any time."

He knew to expect changes to his body as he grew older, but he hadn't seen this one coming.

As his wife drove him home, his body groggy with steroids and Benadryl, he apologized to her for having derailed their day.

"We're in this together," she responded. "I got you. We'll get through this."

It was only then that he understood his wife was giving up shellfish, too.

Life was not always fair, but in that moment, he was deeply grateful that the unfair things were heavily outweighed by the presence of a loving spouse.

THAT TIME IN BAND...
AFTER AMERICAN PIE

The upperclassmen sat at the back of the school bus, kissing under the blankets they'd brought for riding home after the band competition. The chaperones sat at the front of the bus talking to each other and the bus driver, spilling the tea about local goings-on. The underclassmen sat in the middle of the bus, headphones over their ears, counting down the days until they would become upperclassmen.

THE ACCIDENTAL MINIMALIST

It took the fires to break him of his addition to collecting things.

THE QUIET STORM WHEN YOU'RE TOO YOUNG FOR A PONCHO

Some songs live only in humid Southern nights, where an old fan sits in an open window in the back of your grandmother's house and dreams of saying hello to your boy's beautiful cousin visiting from Chicago is the only thing on the agenda for the summer break. Even though you never had the courage to speak to her, the songs remind you of the time you could have.

THE DOCUMENTARIAN

The funeral director played the documentary she made of her life at her memorial service. Up until that moment, none of her family or friends had known she was a filmmaker. Through their grief, though, they slowly understood her last gift to them: she would always be there, if they needed her.

FORGOTTEN BOOK

The interviewer asked him what was his favorite of the books he had written.

He replied that he didn't know, although he knew which one was the most important. It was a thin, forgotten book that everyone had ignored, but it had given him the freedom to become the writer he was now known to be.

THE FILMMAKER

The best films were the ones that made him forget he was watching a film at all. Those were the ones that reminded him of why he made films in the first place.

WHEN A PHONE TAKES SIDES

His disproportionate number of butt calls led him to conduct an experiment. He laid his phone on the counter and gently placed a sheet of paper towel over it. It immediately called his ex-girlfriend and then waited for him to say something that might have been incriminating, had there been anything left to say.

ARMCHAIR

She sits inside her head, analyzing the world around her and developing theories about how it works. She is philosophizing in a vacuum, considerations of other philosophers absent, interactions with the world absent, but her mind present, alone, content with itself, divorced from everything else, the lenses through which she sees the world firmly in place—for now.

MIDNIGHT TALK
A HAIKU

Her whispers tickle his ear like a baby's foot brushed by a feather.

MUSING #5

Sometimes it feels like there's an aching loneliness at the heart of Luther Vandross's music that effectively masquerades as love ballads.

THE YEAR THE MUSIC DIED

Sometimes the tragedy of their deaths shrouded their music in a melancholy that made it difficult to enjoy it the same way ever again.

THE LOVE STORY POEM

He found himself unable to write a love story where the lovers didn't somehow leave the ground—fly—becoming satellites of Blackness, silhouetted against the plenilune, the soundtracks of Afrosurrealism and Afrofuturism converging like Jupiter and Saturn or a DJ's fingers against rings of vinyl that crackled like milk-soaked puffed rice in the bowl of an eight-year-old on a Saturday morning in June.

THE KIDS OF SUMMER
IN MEMORY OF CHRIS KILGORE

Playing two-hand touch in the streets, light pole to light pole, the big kids quarterbacking, the youngsters running long routes, dreams of being Jerry Rice in their heads, the Nerf ball sailing a mile, tight spiral, into the arms of a kid who dropped three passes earlier, but none of that matters now, as both teams celebrate, and the traffic on the block respectfully comes to a halt, allowing the moment to resonate and reach the fingertips of a writer forty years later.

EVERYONE COULD DO IT

If it were really that easy....

THE LEASH

The leash was there only for appearances. There was no way the child could possibly control the beast if it wanted to *go wild*, but the leash gave passersby the ability to believe, if they were so inclined, that the child was the one who was in control.

FOOTNOTES FROM LOST CHAPTERS

They won't remember each other's name in the years that follow, having only a vague recollection of their evening together at a house party thrown by a mutual friend whose name, like their own, is lost to time.

DAYDREAM BELIEVER

She knows they are just *friends* and that they are not *serious*, but she can't help wondering what would happen if they allowed it to be more. In her mind they could make the leap, but she fears that he might feel betrayed and end everything. She'd rather have him like this, than not at all, so she will keep these thoughts to herself and understand that she is both the daydream believer *and* the homecoming queen.

WISDOM
A HAIKU

Wisdom is the crown you fashion from the thorns of experiences.

GLISSANDOS

It's a gentle first kiss, completely unexpected, as they stand by the white upright piano, but in that moment, he knows that he is in love.

DAVID LYNCH
FOR TORREY

His film was widely panned by critics and audiences alike, but they didn't understand that he was trying to make good art, not a good film, as it was nearly impossible to do both—and have each be good, that is.

HELIUM

They carried their love in helium heart balloons that they tied to their outside wrists as they walked hand in hand throughout the city. As time passed, his balloon continued to float, nearly pulling his wrist to the sky, but hers began to droop, allowing her wrist to fall. They continued to walk hand in hand, though, their destination now uncertain, their efforts at being polite to the other obscuring the obvious.

MUSING #6

Jazmine Sullivan's "Let It Burn" comes out the gate sounding like a variety of ad libs over After 7's "Ready or Not," but that rawness of emotion, that loose structure, that desire to break free of the interpolated sample is what makes the song slap so hard.

YOU CAN KEEP YOUR TIARA

She had no desire to be a princess. The idea of kissing a frog or a beast was best left to cartoons.

THE MIRROR GUY

The guy in the mirror reminds him that his calves are too small, his chest is a little too loose, his teeth are slightly crooked, and his elbows and knees are darker than they should be. The guy in the mirror wants him to think about these things when he is away from the mirror, but he refuses to. He is more powerful than the guy in the mirror, and he has resolved to leave those critiques on the floor by the mirror, as they have little use in the world beyond it.

He could have stopped creating on day five, but He didn't.

ASS-KICKER OF THE SOUTHERN WILD

As she has grown older, her skin has thinned considerably. She would be the first to say that she's taken it on the chin quite a few times, but now she's tired of being hit. She tells people everyday that they can go to hell, as if she has the power to send them there directly. Her patience has been replaced with gray strands, and the furrow between her brows, she declared, has given her the authority to stop taking shit. So unless you want to get cussed out, I humbly suggest you keep it moving.

THEY PLAYED THE BLUES

I have two former classmates who died the same way: stabbed in the back by their girlfriends. Though both incidents were more than a decade apart, I still find myself drawing correlations between them. They were both in band with me, one on trumpet, the other on saxophone. Our town was small, and murders were extremely rare.

The city I live in now has more crime than my hometown, but yet none of it has touched my family and me, yet hundreds of miles away, these isolated crimes in my hometown are reminding me that these kinds of things can and will happen and that life is a strange animal that fluffs its tangled, matted fur before our eyes in truly strange and mysterious ways.

Dinosaur Mario leaps cacti and pterodactyls, all in vain, as my new high score will soon be interrupted by my laptop's sporadic connection to my office's janky wireless router.

COLD TURKEY
A HAIKU

Every book is his last one, until he starts to write another.

WIDE SHOT

The film professor critiques his "overuse" of drone shots as a lack of diversity in his cinematography, but to him, the world is a tiny place, and the only way to adequately tell its story is to show it from a distance, like William Anders* gazing through the window of his soul.

---

* William Anders was an astronaut on Apollo 8 and is credited with taking the "Earthrise" photo, the first photo of Earth from space.

INVISIBLE BOOKS

Because ebooks don't take up physical space in her apartment, they are invisible. E-reader storage is something that is ethereal, numbers in space, space of which there is plenty (or so she has been told), so she collects as many books as she can, like a child spinning around in January trying to eat as many snowflakes as she can before they touch the ground.

Watch Hebru draw.

Watch Hebru paint.

Watch Hebru sculpt.

Watch Hebru fly.

THE BLACKNESS WITHIN

The lights are turned off inside the store, but they remain on just outside the entrance. This is to remind people that someone is still paying the electric bill to house the part of the night they are most afraid of.

The storm pleaches the tree branches, reminding me of my grandfather's fingers interlocking right before he gives grace.

MY SISTER AND HER FRIENDS ARE MINIMALISTS

They had nothing, so they made it fashionable.

THE 30-YEAR DEBATE

They would argue about the sound thirty years into their marriage. He claimed the sounds coming from his stomach on their first date were growls of hunger, and she claimed those sounds were gas he was too afraid to let out. Of course she was right (damn you, milk!), but after thirty years, he figured he might as well die on that hill.

AN EXCHANGE IN A BOOKSTORE
FOR ZOË

- What does that say on your t-shirt?

- "It is better to have bought the book than to have read it."

- No, it actually says 'I ♥ NYC.'

- Oh, I thought you were talking about something else.

He had not planned to write so many books. He just had so much to say.

SNOW AND SAND

When she was younger, she loved snow and sand. Now that she was in her forties, she viewed both as nuisances, the snow that seemed to come off in clumps from her boots and the sand that hid between her toes when she got back from the beach. She never stopped to think about the blessings of both, caught too much in the minutiae of her life. Her younger self would not have approved.

The monsters no longer hang out under my bed now that I am an adult.

I miss them.

UNSOLICITED ADVICE

His uncle had told him that it was important to break up with his girlfriend before Christmas, Valentine's Day, or her birthday—whichever was closer—if he wanted to save money.

He didn't realize his uncle had been joking.

OUTSIDE THE GYM

The white kid said he was only playing with the box cutter at school and that he didn't realize it was open when he approached the Black kid.

No, he wasn't going to do anything to anyone, even if another kid hadn't shown up to spook him.

And, no, he was unaware there were rumors the Black kid he had approached had been dating a white girl that he liked.

MUSING #7

Asking me how long does it take for me to remember that I am Black in America when I wake up in the morning is like asking me how many licks does it take to get to the center of a Tootsie Roll pop.

ANTI-LITERACY LAWS

He closed his eyes and tried to imagine the first of his ancestors to pick up a pencil and write in English for the first time in this country. He couldn't fathom the amount of courage that act must have taken. He promised not to forget that as he wrote his own stories.

THINKING OF MEAT MUMMA

She talked about the her novel for decades, collecting notes and clippings, bits of dialogue here and there, her fire for the plot burning ferociously as if soaked in gasoline. Even as her body was preparing to shake its mortal coil, she talked about her characters, poking and prodding them to reveal themselves to her to write down, and for all of this desire to put her story out into the world, Death eventually caught up to her, and it took her hand gently, whispering to her, "Sometimes its the journey of creating art that matters more than the art itself."

OSTENTATION

She sometimes titles her poems with foreign words, feeling a different tongue adds further gravity to her pieces, but they, too, are simply words spoken by humans, wrapped in all their flaws, evolving like the words of her poems—or any words for that matter.

#MUSING #8
A HAIKU

Music is the time machine that allows us to visit memories.

THE CALLBACK
FOR ZOË

They drove down the highway playing her favorite song, and as she began to sing, he stopped her.

"What are you singing?"

"The lyrics."

"But those aren't the lyrics. She's saying, 'Can I look into your eyes?' not 'banana cream pies.'"

"Oh, I thought you were talking about something else."

PART FOUR

T-REX STRESS

The dinosaur stumbles, feet dragging through pixelled dust, eyes fixed on the cactus that never moves. The gamer fumbles with the spacebar, completely disconnected. Every jump a failure, the dinosaur now wondering with a heavy heart how it came to be in hands of someone so unskilled.

STATIC LITERATURE

She taught from only the literature she read up until her dissertation defense, figuring she had read everything of value in her field. She never stopped to consider that the last of those books was published over 40 years ago.

WRITER'S BLOCK

She has convinced herself that there is no such thing as writer's block, so she continues to write daily. Her best friend, however, has convinced herself that writer's block is real and has not written a single creative word in over two years.

THE RECONTEXTUALIZATION
OF A MOMENT IN TIME

Love has wings and must fly.

Lust does not have wings, but it pretends that it does.

BACKGROUND TRACK

Her daughter likes to commandeer the music in the car and listen to her favorite playlists, and as soon as a song starts, she begins to immediately talk over it, telling stories about her friends at school, only to pause at the climax of her story, as if stricken mute, then sing the hook of the song playing in the background, before returning to her story, as if nothing unusual had even occurred.

DORM DEMOLITION

Nearly three quarters of the guys who had lived in Mullen Hall were there the day it was torn down, it's land to now be used for a science building named after someone who'd never attended the college. Though it had been years (many years for some), the men felt like a part of their memories were blasted into infinity with each pass of the wrecking ball, bathrooms where many of them had gotten their hair cut, dorm rooms that had seen late night studying, camaraderie, and even the occasional piece of ass, all of it now lying in pile of rubble, jagged, chalky moments forever lost to time, the men silently taking it in, all of them bound by something far greater than what lay before them.

DREAMS OF A BICYCLE

Some nights he has dreams that he is riding a children's bicycle down the highway to get to the next town, where someone patiently awaits him. Other nights he dreams he is taking a train to the airport and is on the verge of being late for his flight. If he misses it, he will have to ride this bicycle to wherever he must go.

It has been years since he has ridden any kind of bicycle, but he is undaunted by this (at least in his dreams), as it is the transportation he feels he can best control, even if it will require him to to churn one pedal at a time.

SAFARI THROUGH HELL

He is riding on a train across the vastness of fields, but there are hideous beasts lined along the path of the train, many of them curled up in sleeping positions, their beastly children resting nearby. At some point the train will awaken some of the beasts, who will then charge the train. He anticipates this, wanting to go faster, wanting to escape this nightmare, but the train takes its sweet time stirring his illusory peace into a thick cacophonous, gelatinous glob of fear, where it sits at the pit of his soul like the devil's anchor.

EGYPTIAN MUSK

He massages her back with warm oils he purchased from an African street vendor in Little Five Points, kneading her soft bare skin, its warmth electrifying his fingertips, her muscles sliding beneath his thumbs and forefingers. He wants so badly to place kisses along the trail that leads to the small of her back, but this moment, at least for him, is about restraint, about pleasuring her, about being present in this moment and not skipping ahead to the next thing, whatever that might be.

TIME WILL REVEAL

Her son finds the letter tucked in the back of an old yearbook she has not opened in nearly thirty years. He reads it, amazed by the level of adoration expressed toward his mother, realizing that at one time his mother was his age and that a man truly loved her the way he had always hoped his mother would be loved. What happened, he asks her, but what he really asking is why was this man not his father, and she ponders the same thing, now that time has revealed the wisdom of her mistakes.

AUSTERE
A HAIKU

I wish I could laugh at myself, like a baby pooting in the tub.

Before Stevie Wonder sampled Denise Huxtable, he sampled Deniece Williams and created a masterpiece of 80's soul music.

MORNING MEDITATION

He has decided to journal each morning for twenty minutes or so. He will empty his thoughts onto a blank page, then put down his pen and close his journal. As the day goes on, his mental queue will refill, and when the following morning arrives, he will open his journal, take his pen, and attempt to repeat this process, hoping it will become easier each time.

He barely noticed when the hair on his hands became long and thick or when his fingers began to fuse together or when his nails became claws or when his speech became unintelligible or when he began to think of the world as his own, a place to rub his back against and lounge about licking his fur.

One friend tells him to write a story about loss.

Another tells him to write a story about love.

Another tells him to write a story about crime.

He has not ruled out their recommendations, but if he were to do any of them, he'd have to do them his way, which means the stories would need to slant in such a way readers would have to tilt their heads to read them.

PUPPY LOVE

Back in the days before social media—or even the Internet—an industrious teenager would learn the names of the parents of the girl he liked, then look up that number in the phonebook. He'd sit on it for a couple of weeks, working up the nerve to actually dial it and ask to speak to her. If he was lucky enough to get her on the phone, he had to find a way to keep her on the phone (the length of the call would be the gage for how much she was feeling him). The phone calls would lead to hand-written letters passed on to her in the hall with hopes of dancing with her at the homecoming dance hosted at the national guard armory. Maybe he'd get a chance to slow dance with her to Bobby Brown's "Roni," and maybe he'd get a peck on the lips before the lights came up and his older cousin came to pick him up. Then he'd get home and try to sneak a phone call to her on the only phone in the house, hoping his mother didn't wake up and tell him to get off the phone and take his ass to bed. And that night, still replaying all of it in his head, he'd go to sleep, his heart full, damn near overflowing, with something the grown folks liked to call "puppy love."

THE BEGINNING OF THE STORY

He noticed her sitting outside the bookstore, Yaa Gyasi's *Homegoing* opened on the table before her, her toned legs, peeking out from her linen shorts, one crossed over the other, a sandal dangling from a pedicured foot, her eyes intense, her lips on the edge of a smile, her hair resting gently on her shoulders, a true and stunning study in Black beauty. She didn't notice him, but eventually she would. This would be the beginning of their story, the one they would share with others in the decades to follow.

MUSING #9

How long should a great TV show run before it concludes?

The Sopranos did six seasons.

Breaking Bad and *The Wire* did five seasons.

Atlanta did four.

Of course there are shows that have been running more than twenty seasons, but how far have those shows evolved from their origins?

Maybe four to six is best in the end.

THE DINOSAUR (2025)
AFTER AUGUSTO MONTERROSO

The dinosaur watched her curiously as she awoke.

PAPER PLANES

The little boy folds the paper carefully, each crease a prayer whispered into the wind. His tiny plane is fragile, a slip of hope against a vast blue sky.

He looks up, imagining the flight—over oceans, past clouded mountains, into the warmth of St. Lucia, where his father waits by the shore.

The little boy launches it, the plane tumbling into the air, a brief flutter of possibility. He watches it drift, and for a moment, believes that somehow, somewhere, it might land upon his father's hands.

EARLINE'S USED AND RARE BOOKS

The musty smell of old books hung in the summer air as if sprayed from the canister of an air freshener.

"Leave me here," she said, staring at the maze of books that lay ahead.

Her parents, eager to go to the store next door, contemplated this a beat longer than they should've.

"You go ahead," the mother told the father. "I'll hang back and let her look around."

He looked at the excitement in his daughter's eyes. "No, that's all right. We'll all stay."

WHEN LOVE IS A SEED
A HAIKU

His lips, still wet from her kiss, sense a loneliness they have never known.

On the screen, villainous men in their white hats struggle beneath the weight of the horses on their backs, the horses' hooves pulling back the reins to reveal the men's teeth and crooked, forced grins. Behind them, the heroes in black hats, chase them, horses on their backs, forcing them to a crawl.

The little boy watches the television screen, wide-eyed, from his den, enjoying a world that is now upside down.

THE HEAVEN WE CREATE

The couple, their brown skin kissed by time, sits in the rocking chairs on the porch, staring out into the melting horizon. They sip their sweet tea slowly, tasting both the past and the promise of tomorrow. Their memories are quiet whispers, but hope, still tender, sways gently like jasmine in the autumn breeze.

THE DEATH OF A COMPUTER

Hands trembling, he swung the hammer like Thor, and in a single moment, the keys shattered, the computer's screen cracking like an egg in a failed children's physics experiment. The room went silent, and when he picked up his pen, the room began to breathe again, but this time a bit differently.

CHOCOLATE DREAMS

He dreams of diving into a chocolate ocean, and with every stroke, he takes a gulp. He will be like Augustus Gloop*, except completely unchecked, and at some point his brown skin and the brown chocolate will become one, and he will taste himself and rejoice in how delicious he has become.

---

* Augustus Gloop was a character from Roald Dahl's *Charlie and the Chocolate Factory*. He made his exit from the story after drinking from Willy Wonka's liquid chocolate supply, a huge no-no.

META NONSENSE

She writes about a character who is writing about her, and the story flashes for a moment in its meta-ness, then collapses when the *her* character her character is writing about suddenly has writer's block, just like the character, just like herself.

LAURIE LIPTON

Pencil-drawn nightmares, beautiful and tragic, unsettling and repulsive, line the canvas, a tortuous ode to monochromatic surrealism, a thousand whispers of the ghosts that ~~haunt~~ hunt us like we are somnambulistic bovines. We should not be perfect. We should be perfectly afraid.

DONALD GLOVER

There is nothing childish about dreaming while you're awake, your eyes cast toward a violet sky, piercing itself between oranges that hang like planets in their own galaxy far, far away, thinking of a melody or a line of dialogue or a joke or a multi-layered visual expression on how to make Blackness even more spectacularly surreal.

A LOVE STORY, A GHOST STORY, OR BOTH

Shortly after midnight, he awoke to find she was still there and that she had moved even closer.

ON BREATHING AGAIN

Maybe it was the fact that the hole in his belt had simply given out from too many wears. Maybe it was the fact that the belt, while appearing to be leather, was anything but and destined for a short life. Maybe it was the fact that the weight he'd gained caused too much tension. Or Maybe it was because his guardian angel knew he wasn't trying to kill himself. Whatever it was, he was grateful to have been spared the embarrassment of having his mother find him like that, his secret exposed like some tawdry thing she would have to handle with two fingers held at arms length, a disgusting disgrace.

BULLETS IN THE SUBWAY

I am riding a subway through time to stop the other me. He is trying to prevent the deaths of two Black men by transit cops. I understand this, and it pains me that this will happen, but we must allow history to go unchanged, which is why I am chasing myself. Without the first murder in 1968[*], we would have no Afrosurrealism[†]. Without the second murder in 2009[‡], Wakanda[§] would never inspire little Black children around the world to pursue greatness. The other me knows that Black men should not have to die for art, but *I* under-

---

[*] Henry Dumas was murdered in New York City
[†] Dumas was a pioneer in Afrosurrealism, much of his work published posthumously with the guidance of Dr. Eugene Redmond and championed by his editor at the time, the eventual Nobel Prize-winner Toni Morrison
[‡] Oscar Grant was murdered in Oakland, California
[§] Ryan Coogler's first film, *Fruitvale Station*, was based on the murder of Oscar Grant. The critical acclaim of that film provided the opportunity for Coogler to direct *Creed*, then eventually *Black Panther*.

stand that often those sacrifices will ultimately change the world, or so I pray.

EVERY STORY

My teacher told me that every story is about love, whether it be love of the community, love of nature or an ultimate reality, or love of a romantic kind. It sounds nice to hear her say that, to believe that every story shares this common thread, but I know, not so deep down, that she is wrong and that stories are far more nuanced than that, and sometimes love is simply not there. Maybe one could say every story is about something else, but why overgeneralize when you don't have to?

A STUDY IN IRONY

After the bird droppings struck his baseball cap, his wife turned to him and told him that it was good luck.

DECEMBER 6TH

"Mama, my feet still hurt. Can we *please* take the bus today?"

Her mother cut her eyes at her. "Not until Rev. King and Rev. Abernathy say so.*"

It was years ago when her mother, who had since gone home to glory, had told her that. She didn't know at the time they would walk for a couple more months before the car pool picked up enough for her to get a ride to school. It would take over a year for the boycott to end.

They had changed history, and she remembered everything, even if some of the young people nowadays shrugged their shoulders and took it for granted. That didn't mean it wasn't real, that it didn't happen.

---

* The Montgomery Bus Boycott began on December 5, 1955. This story begins on the following day.

BLACK GIRL SCIENCE

She became interested in science by reading about the heroic pursuits of Marvel's RiRi Williams and Lunella Lafayette, Black girl scientists who happened to be heroes. As she grew older, she read about Katharine Johnson, Mary Williams, Mae Jemison, and Kizzmekia Corbett, real-life heroes. Now, as she sits in her dorm room in Abby Hall, tucked quietly at the back of Spelman's campus, she hones her own superpowers in hopes of carrying on the tradition of inspiring the next generation of Black girls.

ATTEMPTED ASSASSINATION
A HAIKU AFTER WYCLEF JEAN

She aimed her bullet for his heart and missed by a mile.

He was too quick.

BLACK MIRROR

Technology smashes its face against the mirror, shattering it, an anthropomorphic smile left in its wake to remind us that it has no intentions of ever losing.

SENDING MESSAGES IN THE EARLY 90S

They'd page each other back and forth with 143[*] and 69[†], two messages they'd said so frequently to each other that they didn't even need to send them as messages, but if you were going to carry a pager, you'd may as well use it.

---

[*] I love you
[†] You already know

IT LOVES ME

In lieu of taking his annual vacation in Rio de Janeiro, he used the money to purchase an AI-enhanced robot that looked Brazilian and did everything his Brazilian escort would have done, or so he preferred to believe. The best part, though, was that he would have the robot year round rather than one week out of the year. Deep down he knew a robot could not replace a woman, but he was just enough of a technophile to convince himself that it would.

ETHER

The laptop screen dies, and his pages dissolve into nothingness. The words still linger in the air, but the story is now gone, swallowed by silence. He wants to scream, to mourn this loss, but he must accept that the book was never his, only borrowed from the ether, a place from which it has now returned.

The tour represented 40 years of their being a singing group. At this point, it was irrelevant whether or not they liked each other. This journey of life required that they move through it together. They would always be able to eat as a group, not so much as individuals. In retrospect, they wonder if their lives might have been vastly different if they hadn't made this career choice when they were only twelve.

FLOWERS
A HAIKU

The flowers make her sneeze, but she prefers them to artificial ones.

WE LIVE IN BROOKLYN, BABY
IN MEMORY OF ROY AYERS

Fresh transplant, but the roots are taking hold, brownstones singing to a part of his soul that once looked at him from album covers, neighbors from the West Indies or the South, callaloo and cornbread, beautiful brown smiles, home in the sunshine. No more searching.

BROTHA
IN MEMORY OF ANGIE STONE

If only America looked at Black men the way that Angie Stone did.

KILLING ME
A HAIKU IN MEMORY OF ROBERTA FLACK

She sings my life with her pain. Melodies linger ghost-like from strummed strings.

BLOOD, SWEAT, AND TEARS

209

She makes it look easy, mainly because she was told that it was a sign of skill to make something complex look simple, so her fans will never see the bruises of her struggle because those secrets are kept behind closed doors, where the floor remains damp with blood, sweat, and tears.

BLACK AND WHITE

He prefers black and white to sepia. He'd rather have no color than be teased with possibilities of what he can never have.

MUSING #10

They used to happen in threes. Now it seems like Death has stopped counting.

THE NIGHT BEFORE THE END OF THE WORLD

He was surprised at how seamlessly the Montblanc severed the umbilical cord of his laptop and set him free.

ACKNOWLEDGMENTS

Special thanks to Elle and Zoë, Torrey, and the Dumas Collective. It's been a wild ride.

ABOUT THE AUTHOR

Ran Walker (he/him) is the author of over 35 books. His short stories, flash fiction, microfiction, and poetry have appeared in a variety of anthologies and journals. Prior to becoming a writer and educator, he worked in magazine publishing and practiced law in Mississippi.

He is the winner of the Indie Author Project's 2019 National Indie Author of the Year Award, the 2019 Black Caucus of the American Library Association Best Fiction Ebook Award, the 2018 Virginia Indie Author Project Award for Adult Fiction, and the 2021 Blind Corner Afrofuturism Microfiction Contest. Ran is an Associate Professor of English and Creative Writing at Hampton University and teaches with Writer's Digest University. He lives in Virginia with his wife and much better half, Lauren, and his amazing daughter, Zoë.

The Golden Book: A 50-Year Marriage Told In 50-Word Stories

Keep It 100: 100-Word Stories

A Burst of Gray: A Novel In 100-Word Stories

The Library of Afro Curiosities: 100-Word Stories

Black Marker: A Novel in 100-Word Stories

GloKat and the Art of Timing: A Novel in 100-Word Stories

A Different Kind of Christmas Story: A Carol in 100-Word Stories

Spaceships Don't Come Equipped with Rearview Mirrors: 50-Word Stories

This Is Not a Poem/Story: 100-Word Stories

Parts of Speech: 100-Word Stories

Four Suits: A Deck of 100-Word Stories

O'ahu: Prose Poems

Apollo's Toy Box

Gods Among Men

One Hundred Ways: A Handbook for Writing 100-Word Stories

Sneaker Marauders: Poems (with Van G. Garrett)

The Night Before the End of the World

www.ingramcontent.com/pod-product-compliance
Lightning Source LLC
Chambersburg PA
CBHW060400310726